Can I Be Good?

Can I Be Good?

LIVINGSTON TAYLOR
Illustrated by TED RAND

Gulliver Books
Harcourt Brace & Company
San Diego   New York   London

Printed in Singapore

I'm a big dog
But I'm not very old
I try very hard
To do just as I'm told.
I wish all the time
I could do what I should,
But it's awfully hard to be good.

Can I be good now?
It's going to be hard.
I'll need some help
To get out in the yard.

Everyone's sleeping,
It's quarter to six,
So when I start howling
I'll be in a fix.
It's terribly hard to be good.

Can I be good now?
Maybe not yet.
It's raining outside
And I've gotten all wet.

I'm shaking water
All over the place,
And the people I live with
Have frowns on their faces.
Sometimes it's hard to be good.

Can I be good now?
I love to play ball.
The garbageman says,
"One toss and that's all!"
I want to play.
He needs to go.
So I bark and I whine
Till he gives one more throw.
I'd rather play ball than be good.

Can I be good now?
The bus has arrived.
I jump right aboard,
My friends are inside.

SCHOOL DISTRICT NO 400

When I run down the aisle
They scream and they shout,
And the crabby bus driver
Yells, "Get that dog out!"
And I was just trying to be good.

Can I be good now?
There's nothing to do.
I'm home all alone
And I'm feeling quite blue.

Chewing a shoe
Will help pass the time.
The new ones taste best,
I hope Dad won't mind.
He knows that I mean to be good.

Can I be good now?
Here comes a white truck
All full of ice cream—
More good doggie luck.

When the ice cream starts dripping,
I get to work quick.
I clean up small faces
With big doggie licks.
It tastes too good to be good.

Can I be good now?
The sun has just set.
I'm so very hungry
I'm getting upset.
I rattle my dish
All over the floor.
But feeding the dog
Is just one more chore.
It can be **so** hard to be good.

Can I be good now?
It's finally time.
I'm fed and I'm full
And feeling just fine.
They're petting my fur
And giving me hugs.
And I'm all bedded down
On my favorite rug.
Finally it's time to be good.

To my wife, Maggie, whose perfect
organization makes simple
thought possible

—L. T.

To my daughter,
Theresa Jane

—T. R.

Library of Congress Cataloging-in-Publication Data
Taylor, Livingston.
Can I be good?/by Livingston Taylor;
illustrated by Ted Rand—1st ed.
p.   cm.
"Gulliver books."
Summary: Although he wants to be good, a big dog keeps doing
things that get him into trouble.
ISBN 0-15-200436-X
[1. Dogs—Fiction. 2. Behavior—Fiction. 3. Stories in rhyme.]
I. Rand, Ted, ill. II. Title.
PZ8.3.T2157Can   1993
[E]—dc20   92-23193

First edition

A B C D E

The illustrations in this book were done in traditional watercolor,
liquid dye, ground chalk, and Prismacolor pencil on 100% rag
cold-press board.
The display type was set in Barcelona by Thompson Type,
San Diego, California.
The text type was set in Minister Light by Central Graphics,
San Diego, California.
Color separations by Bright Arts, Ltd., Singapore
Printed and bound by Tien Wah Press, Singapore
Production supervision by Warren Wallerstein and Ginger Boyer
Designed by Lydia D'moch